Psichopath

Psichopath

Randall Garrett

ÆGYPAN PRESS

Special thanks to Sankar Viswanathan, Greg Weeks, and the
Online Distributed Proofreading Team, which can be found
at http://www.pgdp.net.

This text was reproduced from *Analog Science Fact & Fiction*
October 1960 1960, where it appeared as a work by Darrel T.
Langart.

Psichopath
A publication of
ÆGYPAN PRESS

www.aegypan.com

Given psi powers like clairvoyance and telepathy, solving problems of sabotage would be easy, of course. That is, it seems that way at first thought!

*T*he man in the pastel blue topcoat walked with steady purpose, but without haste, through the chill, wind-swirled drizzle that filled the air above the streets of Arlington, Virginia. His matching blue cap-hood was pulled low over his forehead, and the clear, infrared radiating face mask had been flipped down to protect his chubby cheeks and round nose from the icy wind.

No one noticed him particularly. He was just another average man who blended in with all the others who walked the streets that day. No one recognized him; his face did not appear often in public places, except in his own state, and, even so, it was a thoroughly ordinary face. But, as he walked, Senator John Peter Gonzales was keeping a mental, fine-webbed, four-dimensional net around him, feeling for the slightest touch of recognition. He wanted no one to connect him in any way with his intended destination.

It was not his first visit to the six-floor brick building that stood on a street in a lower-middle-class district of Arlington. Actually, government business took him there more often than would have been safe for the average man-on-the-street. For Senator Gonzales, the process of remaining incognito was so elementary that it was almost subconscious.

Arriving at his destination, he paused on the sidewalk to light a cigarette, shielding it against the wind and drizzle with cupped hands while his mind made one last check on the surroundings. Then he strode quickly up the five steps to the double doors which were marked: *The Society For Mystical And Metaphysical Research, Inc.*

Just as he stepped in, he flipped the face shield up and put on an old-fashioned pair of thick-lensed, black-rimmed spectacles. Then, his face assuming a bland smile that would have been completely out of place on Senator Gonzales, he went from the foyer into the front office.

"Good afternoon, Mrs. Jesser," he said, in a high, smooth, slightly accented voice that was not his own. "I perceive by your aura that you are feeling well. Your normal aura-color is tinged with a positive golden hue."

Mrs. Jesser, a well-rounded matron in her early forties, rose to the bait like a porpoise being hand-fed at a Florida zoo. "*Dear* Swami Chandra! How perfectly wonderful to see you again! You're looking *very* well your-*self.*"

The Swami, whose Indian blood was of the Aztec rather than the Brahmin variety, nonetheless managed to radiate all the mystery of the East. "My well-being, dear Mrs. Jesser, is due to the fact that I have been communing for the past three months with my very good friend, the Fifth Dalai Lama. A most refreshingly wise person." Senator Gonzales was fond of the Society's crackpot receptionist, and he knew exactly what kind of hokum would please her most.

"Oh, I *do* hope you will find time to tell me *all* about it," she said effusively. "Mr. Balfour isn't in the city just now," she went on. "He's lecturing in New York on the history of flying saucer sightings. Do you realize that this is the fortieth anniversary of the first saucer sighting, back in 1944?"

"The first *photographed* sighting," the Swami corrected condescendingly. "Our friends have been watching and guiding us for far longer than that, and were sighted many times before they were photographed."

Mrs. Jesser nodded briskly. "Of course. You're right, as always, Swami."

"I am sorry to hear," the Swami continued smoothly, "that I will not be able to see Mr. Balfour. However, I came at the call of Mr. Brian Taggert, who is expecting me."

Mrs. Jesser glanced down at her appointment sheet. "He didn't mention an appointment to me. However —" She punched a button on the intercom. "Mr. Taggert? Swami Chandra is here to see you. He says he has an appointment."

Brian Taggert's deep voice came over the instrument. "The Swami, as usual, is very astute. I have been thinking about calling him. Send him right up."

"You may go up, Swami," said Mrs. Jesser, wide-eyed. She watched in awe as the Swami marched regally through the inner door and began to climb the stairs toward the sixth floor.

One way to hide an ex-officio agency of the United States Government was to label it truthfully — *The Society For Mystical And Metaphysical Research*. In spite of the fact that the label was literally true, it sounded so crackpot that no one but a crackpot would bother to look into it. As a consequence, better than ninety percent of the membership of the Society was composed of just such people. Only a few members of the "core" knew the organization's true function and purpose. And as long as such scatter-brains as Mrs. Jesser and Mr. Balfour were in there pitching, no one would ever penetrate to the actual core of the Society.

The senator had already pocketed the exaggerated glasses by the time he reached the sixth floor, and his face had lost its bland, overly-wise smile. He pushed open the door to Taggert's office.

"Have you got any ideas yet?" he asked quickly.

Brian Taggert, a heavily-muscled man with dark eyes and black, slightly wavy hair, sat on the edge of a couch in one corner of the room. His desk across the room was there for paperwork only, and Taggert had precious little of that to bother with.

He took a puff from his heavy-bowled briar. "We're going to have to send an agent in there. Someone who can be on the spot. Someone who can get the feel of the situation first hand."

"That'll be difficult. We can't just suddenly stick an unknown in there and have an excuse for his being there. Couldn't Donahue or Reeves —"

Taggert shook his head. "Impossible, John. Extrasensory perception can't replace sight, anymore than sight can replace hearing. You know that."

"Certainly. But I thought we could get enough information that way to tell us who our saboteur is. No dice, eh?"

"No dice," said Taggert. "Look at the situation we've got there. The purpose of the Redford Research Team is to test the Meson Ultimate Decay Theory of Dr. Theodore Nordred. Now, if we —"

Senator Gonzales, walking across the room toward Taggert, gestured with one hand. "I know! I know! Give me *some* credit for intelligence! But we *do* have one suspect, don't we? What about *him?*"

Taggert chuckled through a wreath of smoke. "Calm down, John. Or are you trying to give me your impression of Mrs. Jesser in a conversation with a saucerite?"

The senator laughed and sat down in a nearby chair. "All right. Sorry. But this whole thing is lousing up our entire space program. First off, we nearly lose Dr. Ch'ien, and, with him gone, the interstellar drive project would've been shot. Now, if this sabotage keeps up, the Redford project *will* be shot, and that means we might have to stick to the old-fashioned rocket to get off-planet. Brian, we *need* antigravity, and, so far, Nordred's theory is our only clue."

"Agreed," said Taggert.

"Well, we're never going to get it if equipment keeps mysteriously burning itself out, breaking down, and just generally goofing up. This morning, the primary exciter on the new ultracosmotron went haywire, and the beam of sodium nuclei burned through part of the accelerator tube wall. It'll take a month to get it back in working order."

Taggert took his pipe out of his mouth and tapped the dottle into a nearby ash disposal unit. "And you want to pick up our pet spy?"

Senator Gonzales scowled. "Well, I'd certainly call him our prime suspect." But there was a certain lack of conviction in his manner.

Brian Taggert didn't flatly contradict the senator. "Maybe. But you know, John, there's one thing that bothers me about these accidents."

"What's that?"

"The fact that we have not one shred of evidence that points to sabotage."

*I*n a room on the fifth floor, directly below Brian Taggert's office, a young man was half sitting, half reclining in a thickly upholstered adjustable chair. He had dropped the back of the chair to a forty-five degree angle and lifted up the footrest; now he was leaning back in lazy comfort, his ankles crossed, his right hand holding a slowly smoldering cigarette, his eyes contemplating the ceiling. Or, rather, they seemed to be contemplating something *beyond* the ceiling.

It was pure coincidence that the focus of his thoughts happened to be located in about the same volume of space that his eyes seemed to be focused on. If Brian Taggert and Senator Gonzales had been in the room below, his eyes would still be looking at the ceiling.

In repose, his face looked even younger than his twenty-eight years would have led one to expect. His close-cropped brown hair added to the impression of youth, and the well-tailored suit on his slim, muscular body added to the effect. At any top-flight university, he could have passes for a well-bred, sophisticated, intelligent student who had money enough to indulge himself and sense enough not to overdo it.

He was beginning to understand the pattern that was being woven in the room above — beginning to feel it in depth.

Senator Gonzalez was mildly telepathic, inasmuch as he could pick up thoughts in the prevocal stage — the stage at which thought becomes definitely organized into words, phrases, and sentences. He could go a little deeper, into the selectivity stage, where the linking processes of logic took over from the nonlogical but rational processes of the precon-scious — but only if he knew the person well. Where the senator excelled was in detecting emotional tone and manipu-lating emotional processes, both within himself and within others.

Brian Taggert was an analyzer, an originator, a motivator — and more. The young man found himself avoiding too deep a probe into the mind of Brian Taggert; he knew that he had not yet achieved the maturity to understand the multilayered depths of a mind like that. Eventually, perhaps. . . .

Not that Senator Gonzales was a child, nor that he was emotionally or intellectually shallow. It was merely that he was not of Taggert's caliber.

The young man absently took another drag from his cigarette. Taggert had explained the basic problem to him, but he was getting a wider picture from the additional information that Senator Gonzales had brought.

Dr. Theodore Nordred, a mathematical physicist and one of the top-flight, high-powered, original minds in the field, had shown that Einstein's final equations only held in a universe composed entirely of normal matter. Since the great Einstein had died before the Principle of Parity had been overthrown in the mid-fifties, he had been unable to incorporate the information into his Unified Field Theory. Nordred had been able to show, mathematically, that Einstein's equations were valid only for a completely "dexter," or right-handed universe, or for a completely "sinister" or left-handed universe.

Although the universe in which Man lived was predominantly dexter — arbitrarily so designated — it was not completely so. It had a "sinister" component amounting to approximately one one-hundred-thousandth of one percent. On the average, one atom out of every ten million in the universe was an atom of antimatter. The distribution was unequal of course; antimatter could not exist in contact with ordinary matter. Most of it was distributed throughout interstellar space in the form of individual atoms, freely floating in space, a long way from any large mass of normal matter.

But that minute fraction of a percent was enough to show that the known universe was not totally Einsteinian. In a purely Einsteinian universe, antigravity was impossible, but if the equations of Dr. Theodore Nordred were actually a closer approximation to true reality than those of Einstein, then antigravity *might* be a practical reality.

And that was the problem the Redford Research Team was working on. It was a parallel project to the interstellar drive problem, being carried on elsewhere.

*T*he "pet spy," as Taggert had called him, was Dr. Konrad Bern, a middle-aged Negro from Tanganyika, who was convinced that only under Communism could the colored races of the world achieve the technological organization and living standard of the white man. He had been trained as a "sleeper"; not even the exhaustive investigations of the FBI had turned up any relationship between Bern and the Soviets. It had taken the telepathic probing of the S.M.M.R. agents to uncover his real purposes. Known, he constituted no danger.

There was no denying that he was a highly competent, if not brilliant, physicist. And, since it was quite impossible for him to get any information on the Redford Project into the hands of the opposition — it was no longer fashionable to call Communists "the enemy" — there was no reason why he shouldn't be allowed to contribute to the American efforts to bridge space.

Three times in the five months since Bern had joined the project, agents of the Soviet government had made attempts to contact the physicist. Three times the FBI, warned by S.M.M.R. agents, had quietly blocked the contact. Konrad Bern had been effectively isolated.

But, at the project site itself, equipment failure had become increasingly more frequent, all out of proportion to the normal accident rate in any well-regulated laboratory. The work of the project had practically come to a standstill; the ultra-secret project reports to the President were beginning to show less and less progress in the basic research, and more and more progress in repairing damaged equipment. Apparently, though, increasing efficiency in repair work was self-neutralizing; repairing an instrument in half the time merely meant that it could break down twice as often.

It had to be sabotage. And yet, not even the S.M.M.R. agents could find any trace of intentional damage nor any thought patterns that would indicate deliberate damage.

And Senator John Peter Gonzales quite evidently did *not* want to face the implications of *that* particular fact.

"We're going to have to send an agent in," Taggert repeated.

(*That's my cue,* thought the young man on the fifth floor as he crushed out his cigarette and got up from the chair.)

"I don't know how we're going to manage it," said the senator. "What excuse do we have for putting a new man on the Redford team?"

Brian Taggert grinned. "What they need is an expert repair technician — a man who knows how to build and repair complex research instruments. He doesn't have to know anything about the purpose of the team itself, all he has to do is keep the equipment in good shape."

Senator Gonzalez let a slow smile spread over his face. "You've been gulling me, you snake. All right; I deserved it. Tell him to come in."

As the door opened, Taggert said: "Senator Gonzales, may I present Mr. David MacHeath? He's our man, I think."

*D*avid MacHeath watched a blue line wriggle its way erratically across the face of an oscilloscope. "The wave form is way off," he said flatly, "and the frequency is slithering all over the place."

He squinted at the line for a moment then spoke to the man standing nearby. "Signal Harry to back her off two degrees, then run her up slowly, ten minutes at a time."

The other man flickered the key on the side of the small carbide-Welsbach lamp. The shutters blinked, sending pulses of light down the length of the ten-foot diameter glass-walled tube in which the men were working. Far down the tube, MacHeath could see the answering flicker from Harry, a mile and a half away in the darkness.

MacHeath watched the screen again. After a few seconds, he said: "Okay! Hold it!"

Again the lamp flashed.

"Well, it isn't perfect," MacHeath said, "but it's all we can do from here. We'll have to evacuate the tube to get her in perfect balance. Tell Harry to knock off for the day."

While the welcome message was being flashed, MacHeath shut off the testing instruments and disconnected them. It was possible to compensate a little for the testing equipment, but a telephone, or even an electric flashlight, would simply add to the burden.

Bill Griffin shoved down the key on the lamp he was holding and locked it into place. The shutters remained open, and the lamp shed a beam of white light along the shining walls of the cylindrical tube. "How much longer do you figure it'll take, Dave?" he asked.

"Another shift, at least," said MacHeath, picking up the compact, shielded instrument case. "You want to carry that mat?"

Griffin picked up the thick sponge-rubber mat that the instrument case had been sitting on, and the two men started off down the tube, walking silently on the sponge-rubber-soled shoes which would not scratch the glass underfoot.

"Any indication yet as to who our saboteur is?" Griffin asked.

"I'm not sure," MacHeath admitted. "I've picked up a couple of leads, but I don't know if they mean anything or not."

"I wonder if there *is* a saboteur," Griffin said musingly. "Maybe it's just a run of bad luck. It could happen, you know. A statistical run of —"

"You don't believe that, anymore than I do," MacHeath said.

"No. But I find it even harder to believe that a materialistic philosophy like Communism could evolve any workable psionic discipline."

"So do I," agreed MacHeath.

"But it can't be physical sabotage," Griffin argued. "There's not a trace of it — anywhere. It *has* to be psionic."

"Right," said MacHeath, grinning as he saw what was coming next.

"But we've already eliminated that. So?" Griffin nodded firmly as if in full agreement with himself. "So we follow the dictum of the Master: 'Eliminate the impossible; whatever is left, no matter how improbable, is the truth.' And, since there is absolutely nothing left, there is no truth. At the bottom, the whole thing is merely a matter of mental delusion."

"Sherlock Holmes would be proud of you, Bill," MacHeath said. "And so am I."

Griffin looked at MacHeath oddly. "I wish I was a halfway decent telepath, I'd like to know what's going on in your preconscious."

"You'd have to dig deeper than that, I'm afraid," MacHeath said ruefully. "As soon as my subconscious has solved the problem, I'll let you know."

"I've changed my mind," said Griffin cheerfully. "I don't envy your telepathy. I don't envy a guy who has to TP his own subconscious to find out what he's thinking."

MacHeath chuckled softly as he turned the bolt that opened the door in the "gun" end of the stripped-nuclei accelerator. The seals broke with a soft hiss. Evidently, the barometric pressure outside the two-mile-long underground tube had changed slightly during the time they had been down there.

"It'll be a week before we can test it," MacHeath said in a tired voice. "Even after we get it partly in balance. It'll take that long to evacuate the tube and sweep it clean."

*I*t was the first sentence he had spoken in the past hour or so, and it was purely for the edification of the man who was standing on the other side of the air lock, although neither Griffin nor MacHeath had actually seen him as yet.

Griffin was not a telepath in the sense that the S.M.M.R. used the word, but to a non-psionicist, he would have appeared to be one. Membership in the "core" group of the *Society for Mystical and Metaphysical Research* required, above all, *understanding.* And, with that understanding, a conversation between two members need consist only of an occasional gesture and a key word now and then.

The word "understanding" needs emphasis. Without understanding of another human mind, no human mind can be completely effective. Without that understanding, no human being can be completely free.

And yet, the English word "understanding" is only an approximation to the actual process that must take place. *Total* understanding, in one sense, would require that a person actually *become* another person — that he be able to feel, completely and absolutely, every emotion, every thought, every bodily sensation, every twinge of memory, every judgment, every decision, and every sense of personal identity that is felt by the other person, no more and no less.

Such totality is, obviously, neither attainable nor desirable. The result would be a merger of identities, a total unification. And, as a consequence, a complete loss of one of the human beings involved.

Optimum "understanding" requires that a judgment be made, and that, in turn, requires *two* minds — not a fusion of identity. There must be one to judge and another to be judged, and each mind plays both roles.

Love thy neighbor as thyself. But the original Greek word would translate better as "respect and understand" than as the modern English "love." The founders of our modern religions were not fools; they simply did not have the tools at hand to formulate their knowledge properly. As understanding increases, a critical point is reached, which causes a qualitative change in the human mind.

First, self-understanding must come. The human mind operates through similarities, and the thing most similar to any human mind is itself. The next most similar thing is another human mind.

From that point on, all objects, processes, and patterns in the universe can be graded according to their similarity to each other, and, ultimately, to their similarity to the human mind.

Two given entities may seem utterly dissimilar, but they can always be linked by a *tertium quid* — a "third thing" which is similar to both. This third thing, be it a material object or a product of the human imagination, is called a symbol. Symbols are the bridges by which the human mind can reach and manipulate the universe in which it exists. With the proper symbols and the understanding to use them, the human mind is limited only by its own inherent structural restrictions.

One of the most active research projects of the S.M.M.R. was the construction of a more powerful symbology. Psionics had made tremendous strides in the previous four decades, but it was still in the alchemy stage. So far, symbols for various processes could only be worked out by cut-and-try, rule-of-thumb methods, using symbols already established, including languages and mathematics. None were completely satisfactory, but they worked fairly well within their narrow limits.

As far as communication was concerned, the hashed-together symbology used by the S.M.M.R. was better than any conceivable code. The understanding required to "break" the "code" was well beyond the critical point. Anyone who could break it was, *ipso facto*, a member of the S.M.M.R.

Most people didn't even realize that a conversation was taking place between two members, especially if a "cover conversation" was used at the same time.

*M*acHeath's verbal discussion of the testing of the nuclei accelerator was just such a cover. Even before he had cracked the air lock, he had known that Dr. Theodore Nordred was standing on the other side of the thick wall.

MacHeath pushed the heavy door open on its smooth hinges. "Oh, hello, Dr. Nordred. How's everything?"

The heavy-set mathematician smiled pleasantly as MacHeath and Griffin came into the gun chamber. "I just thought I'd come down and see how you were getting along," he said. His voice was a low tenor, with just a touch of Midwestern twang. "Sometimes the creative mind gets bogged down in the nth-order abstractions that have no discernible connection with anything at all." He chuckled. "When that happens, I drop everything and go out to find something mundane to worry about."

Nordred was only an inch shorter than the slim MacHeath, and he weighed in at close to two hundred pounds. At twenty-five, he had had the build of a lightweight wrestler; thirty more years had added poundage — a roll beneath his chin and a bulge at the belly — but he still looked capable of going a round or two without tiring. His shock of heavy hair was a mixture of mouse-brown and grey, and it seemed to have a tendency to stand up on end, which added another inch and a half to his height. His round face had a tendency to smile when he was talking or working with his hands; when he was deep in thought, his face usually relaxed into thoughtful blankness. He frowned rarely, and only for seconds at a time.

"It seems to me you have enough to worry about, doctor," MacHeath said banteringly, "without looking for it." He put down his instrument case and took out a cigarette while Griffin closed the door to the acceleration tube.

"Oh I don't have to look far," Nordred said. "How long do you think it will be before we can resume our work with the Monster?"

"Ten days to two weeks," MacHeath said promptly.

"I see." One his rare frowns crossed his face. "I wish I knew why the exciter arced across. It shouldn't have."

"Don't you have any idea?" MacHeath asked innocently. At the same time, he opened his mind wide to net in every wisp and filament of Nordred's thoughts that he could reach.

"None at all," admitted the mathematician. "Weakness in the insulation, I suppose, though it tested solidly enough." And his mind, as far back as his preconscious and the upper fringes of his subconscious, agreed with his words. MacHeath could go no deeper as yet; he didn't know Nordred well enough yet.

There were suspicions in Nordred's mind that the insulation weakness must have been caused by deliberate sabotage, but he had no one to pin his suspicions on. Neither he nor anyone else connected with the Redford project was aware of the true status of Dr. Konrad Bern.

"Well, let's hope it doesn't happen again," MacHeath said. "Balancing these babies so that they work properly is hard enough for a deuteron accelerator, but the Monster here is ten times as touchy."

Nordred nodded absently. "I know. But our work can't be done with anything less." Nordred actually knew less about the engineering details of the big accelerator than anyone else on the project; he was primarily a philosopher-mathematician, and only secondarily a physicist. He was theoretically in charge of the project, but the actual experimentation was done by the other four men; Drs. Roger Kent, Paul Luvochek, Solomon Bessermann, and Konrad Bern. These four and their assistants set up and ran off the experiments designed to test Dr. Nordred's theories.

MacHeath picked up his instrument case again, and the three men went out of the gun chamber, into the outer room, and then started up the spiral stairway that led to the surface, talking as they went. But the apparent conversation had little to do with the instruction that MacHeath was giving Griffin as they climbed.

So when MacHeath stopped suddenly and patted at his coverall pockets, Griffin was ready for the words that came next.

"Damn!" MacHeath said. "I've left my notebook. Will you go down and get it for me, Bill?"

Dr. Nordred had neither understood nor noticed the actual instructions:

"Bill, as soon as I give you an excuse, get back down there and check that gun chamber. Give it a thorough going-over. I don't really think you'll find a thing, but I don't want to take any chances at this stage of the game."

"Right," said Griffin, starting back down the stairway.

MacHeath and Dr. Nordred went on climbing.

*D*avid MacHeath sat at a table in the project's cafeteria, absently stirring his coffee, and trying to look professionally modest while Dr. Luvochek and Dr. Bessermann alternately praised him for his work.

Luvochek, a tubby little butterball of a man, whose cherubic face would have made him look almost childlike if it weren't for the blue of his jaw, said: "You and those two men of yours have really done a marvelous job in the past four days, Mr. MacHeath — really marvelous."

"I'll say," Bessermann chimed in. "I was getting pretty tired of looking at burned-out equipment and spending three-quarters of my time putting in replacement parts and wielding a soldering gun." Bessermann was leaner than Luvochek, but, like his brother scientist, he was balding on top. Both men were in their middle thirties.

"I don't understand this jinx, myself," Luvochek said. "At first, it was just little things, but the accidents got worse and worse. And then, when the Monster blew —" He stopped and shook his head slowly. "I'd suspect sabotage, except that there was never any sign of tampering with the equipment I saw."

"What do you think of the sabotage idea?" Bessermann asked MacHeath.

MacHeath shrugged. "Haven't seen any signs of it."

"Run of bad luck," said Luvochek. "That's all."

As they talked MacHeath absorbed the patterns of thought that wove in and out in the two men's minds. Both men were more open than Dr. Nordred; they were easier for MacHeath to understand. Nowhere was there any thought of guilt — at least, as far as sabotage was concerned.

MacHeath drank his coffee slowly and thoughtfully, keeping up his part of the three-way conversation while he concentrated on his own problem.

One thing was certain: Nowhere in the minds of any of the personnel of the Redford Project was there any conscious knowledge of sabotage. Not even in the mind of Konrad Bern.

Dr. Roger Kent, a tall, lantern-jawed sad-eyed man in his forties, had been hard to get through to at first, but as soon as MacHeath discovered that the hard block Kent had built up around himself was caused by grief over a wife who had been dead five years, he became as easy to read as a billboard. Kent had submerged his grief in work; the eternal drive of the true scientist to drag the truth out of Mother Nature. He was constitutionally incapable of sabotaging the very instruments that had been built to dig in after that truth.

Dr. Konrad Bern, on the other hand, was difficult to read below the preconscious stage. Science, to him, was a form of power, to be used for "idealistic" purposes. He was perfectly capable of sabotaging the weapons of an enemy if it became necessary, whether that meant ruining a physical instrument or carefully falsifying the results of an experiment. Outwardly, he was a pleasant enough chap, but his mind revealed a rigidly held pattern of hatreds, fears, and twisted idealism. He held them tightly against the onslaughts of a hostile world.

And that meant that he couldn't possibly have any control over whatever psionic powers he may have had.

Unless —

Unless he was so expert and so well-trained that he was better than anything the S.M.M.R. had ever known.

MacHeath didn't even like to think about that. It would mean that all the theory of psionics that had been built up so painstakingly over the past years would have to be junked *in toto.*

Something was gnawing in the depths of his mind. In the perfectly rational but utterly nonlogical part of his subconscious where hunches are built, something was trying to form.

MacHeath didn't try to probe for it. As soon as he had enough information for the hunch to be fully formed, it would be ready to use. Until then, it would be worthless, and probing for it might interrupt the formation.

*H*e was just finishing his coffee as Bill Griffin came in the door and headed toward the table where MacHeath, Luvochek, and Bessermann were sitting.

MacHeath stood up and said: "Excuse me. I'll have to be getting some work done if you guys are ever going to get your own work done."

"Sure."

"Go ahead."

"Thanks for the coffee," MacHeath added as he moved away.

"Anytime," said Bessermann, grinning. "You guys just keep up the good work. When you fix 'em, they stay fixed. We haven't had a burnout since you came."

"Maybe you broke our statistical jinx," said Luvochek, with a chubby smile.

"Maybe," said MacHeath. "I hope so."

For some reason, the gnawing in his hunch factory became more persistent.

As he and Griffin walked toward the door, Griffin reported rapidly. "I checked everything in the gun chamber. No sign of any tampering. Everything's just as we left it. The dust film hasn't been disturbed."

"It figures," said MacHeath.

Outside, in the corridor, they met Dr. Konrad Bern hurrying toward the cafeteria. He stopped as he saw them.

"Oh, hello, Mr. MacHeath, Mr. Griffin," he said. His white-toothed smile was friendly, but both of the S.M.M.R. agents could detect the hostility that was hard and brittle beneath the surface. "I wanted to thank you for the wonderful job you've been doing."

"Why, thank you, doctor," said MacHeath honestly. "We aim to satisfy."

Bern chuckled. "You're doing well so far. Odd streak of luck we've had, isn't it? Poor Dr. Nordred has been under a terrible strain; his whole life work is tied up in this project." He made a vague gesture with one hand. "Would you care for some coffee?"

"Just had some, thanks," said MacHeath, "but we'll take a rain check."

"Fine. Anytime." And he went on into the cafeteria.

"Wow!" said Griffin as he walked on down the corridor with MacHeath. "That man is scared silly! But what an actor! You'd never know he was eating his guts out."

"Sure he's scared," MacHeath said. "With all this sabotage talk going around, he's afraid there'll be an exhaustive investigation, and he can't take that right now."

Griffin frowned. "I guess I missed that. What did you pick up?"

"He's supposed to meet a Soviet agent tonight, and he's afraid he'll be caught. He doesn't know what happened to the first three, and he won't know what will happen to Number Four tonight.

"We'll keep him around as long as he's useful. He's not a Bohr or a Pauli or a Fermi, but he —"

MacHeath stopped himself suddenly and came to a dead halt.

"My God," he said softly, "that's *it.*"

His hunch had hatched.

After a moment, he said: "Harry is getting back from the target end of the tube now, Bill. He can't pick me up, so beetle it down to the tool room, get him, and get up to the workshop fast. If I'm not there, wait; I have a little prying to do."

"Can do," said Griffin. He went toward the elevator at an easy lope.

David MacHeath went in the opposite direction.

*W*hen MacHeath returned to the workshop which he had been assigned, Bill Griffin and Harry Benbow were waiting for him. Beside the big-muscled Griffin, Harry Benbow looked even thinner than he was. He was a good six-two, which made him a head taller than Griffin, but, unlike many tall, lean men, Benbow had no tendency to slouch; he stood tall and straight, reminding MacHeath of a poplar tree towering proudly over the countryside. Benbow was one of those rare American Negroes whose skin was actually as close to being "black" as human pigmentation will allow. His eyes were like disks of obsidian set in spheres of white porcelain, which gave an odd contrast-similarity effect when compared with Griffin's china-blue eyes.

If the average man had wanted to pick two human beings who were "opposites," he could hardly have made a better choice than Benbow and the short, thickly-built, blond-haired, pink-skinned Bill Griffin. But the average man would be so struck by the differences that he would never notice that the similarities were vastly more important.

"You look as if you'd just been kissed by Miss America," Harry said as MacHeath came through the door.

"Better than that," MacHeath said. "We've got work to do."

"What's the pitch?" Griffin wanted to know.

"Well, in the first place, I'm afraid Dr. Konrad Bern is no longer of any use to the Redford Project. We're going to have to arrest him as an unregistered agent of the Soviet Government."

"It's just as well," said Harry Benbow gently. "His research hasn't done us any good and it hasn't done the Soviets any good. The poor guy's been on edge ever since he got here. All the pale hide around this place stirs up every nerve in him."

"What got you onto this?" Griffin asked MacHeath.

"A hunch first," MacHeath said. "Then I got data to back it up. But, first . . . Harry, how'd you know about Bern's reactions? He keeps those prejudices of his down pretty deep; I didn't think you could go that far."

"I didn't have to. He spent half an hour talking to me this morning. He was so happy to see a fellow human being — according to his definition of human being — that he was as easy to read as if *you* were doing the reading."

MacHeath nodded. "I hate to throw him to the wolves, but he's got to go."

"What was the snooping you said you had to do?" Griffin asked.

"Dates. Times. Briefly, I found that the run of accidents has been building up to a peak. At first, it was just small meters that went wrong. Then bigger, more complex stuff. And, finally, the Monster went. See the pattern?"

The other men nodded.

"You're the therapist," Griffin said. "What do you suggest?"

"Shock treatment," said David MacHeath.

*J*ust how Dr. Konrad Bern got wind of the fact that a squad of FBI men had come to the project to arrest him that evening is something that MacHeath didn't know until later. He was busy at the time, ignoring anything but what he was interested in. It always fascinated him to watch the mind of a psychokinetic expert at work. He couldn't do the trick himself, and he was always amazed at the ability of anyone who could.

It was like watching a pianist play a particularly difficult concerto. A person can watch a pianist, see every move he is making, and why he is making it. But being able to see what is going on doesn't mean that one can duplicate the action. MacHeath was in the same position. Telepathically, he could observe the play of emotions that ran through a psychokinetic's mind — the combinations of avid desire and the utter loathing which, playing one against another, could move a brick, a book, or a Buick if the mind was powerful enough. But he couldn't do it himself, no matter how carefully he tried to follow the raging emotions that acted as two opposing jaws of a pair of tongs to lift and move the object.

And so engrossed was he with the process that he did not notice that Konrad Bern had eluded the FBI. He was unaware of what had happened until one of the Federal agents rapped loudly on the workshop door.

Almost instantly, MacHeath picked up the information from the agent's mind. He glanced at Griffin and Benbow. "You two can handle it. Be careful you don't overdo it."

Then he went to the door and opened it a trifle. "Yes?"

The man outside showed a gold badge. "Morgan, FBI. You David MacHeath?"

"Yes." MacHeath stepped outside and showed the FBI man his identification.

"We were told to co-operate with you in this Konrad Bern case. He's managed to slip away from us somehow, but we know he's still in the area. He can't get past the gate."

MacHeath let his mind expand until it meshed with that of Dr. Konrad Bern.

"There is a way out," MacHeath snapped. "The acceleration tube."

"What?"

"Come on!" He started sprinting toward the elevators. He explained to the FBI agent as they went.

"The acceleration tube of the ultracosmotron runs due north of here for two miles underground. The guard at the other end won't be expecting anyone to be coming from the inside of the target building. If Bern plays his cards right, he can get away."

"Can't we phone the target building?" the FBI man asked.

"No. We shut off all the electrical equipment and took down some of the wires so we could balance the acceleration fields."

"Well, if he's on foot, we could send a car out there. We'd get there before he does. Uh . . . wouldn't we?"

"Maybe. But he'll kill himself if he sees he's trapped." That wasn't quite true. Bern was ready to fight to the death, and he had a heavy pistol to back him up. MacHeath didn't want to see anyone killed, and he didn't want stray bullets flying around the inside of that tube or in the target room.

MacHeath and the FBI agent piled out of the elevator at the bottom of the shaft. Dr. Roger Kent was standing at the head of the stairs that spiraled down to the gun chamber. Dr. Kent knew that Bern had gone down the stairway, but he didn't know why.

"He's our saboteur," MacHeath said quickly. "I'm going after him. As soon as I close the door and seal it, you turn on the pumps. Lower the air pressure in the tube to a pound per square inch below atmospheric. That'll put a force of about a ton and a quarter against the doors, and he won't be able to open them."

Dr. Kent still didn't grasp the fact that Bern was a spy.

"Explain to him, Morgan," MacHeath told the Federal agent. He went on down the spiral staircase, knowing that Kent would understand and act in plenty of time.

*T*he door to the tube was standing open. MacHeath slipped on a pair of the sponge-soled shoes, noticing angrily that Bern hadn't bothered to do so. He went into the tube and closed the door behind him. Then he started down the blackness of the tube at a fast trot. Ahead of him, in the utter darkness, he could hear the click of heels as the leather-shod Bern moved toward the target end of the long tube.

Neither of them had lights. They were unnecessary, for one thing, since there was only one direction to go and there were no obstacles in the path. Bern would probably have carried a flashlight if he'd been able to get his hands on one quickly, but he hadn't, so he went in darkness. MacHeath didn't want a light; in the darkness, he had the advantage of knowing where his opponent was.

Every so often, Bern would stop, listening for sounds of pursuit, since his own footsteps, echoing down the glass-lined cylinder, drowned out any noise from behind. But MacHeath, running silently on the toes of his thick-soled shoes, kept in motion, gaining on the fleeing spy.

A two-mile run is a good stretch of exercise for anyone, but MacHeath didn't dare slow down. As it was, Konrad Bern was already tugging frantically at the door that led to the target room by the time MacHeath reached him. But the faint sighing of the pumps had already told MacHeath that the air pressure had been dropped. Bern couldn't possibly get the door open.

MacHeath's lungs wanted to be filled with air; his chest wanted to heave; he wanted to pant, taking in great gulps of life-giving oxygen. But he didn't dare. He didn't want Bern to know he was there, so he strained to keep his breath silent.

He stepped up behind the physicist in the pitch blackness, and judging carefully, brought his fist down on the nape of the man's neck in a hard rabbit punch.

Konrad Bern dropped unconscious to the floor of the tube.

Then MacHeath let his chest pump air into his lungs in long, harsh gasps. Shakily, he lowered himself to the floor beside Bern and squatted on his haunches, waiting for the hiss of the bleeder valve that would tell him that the air pressure had been raised to allow someone to enter the air lock.

It was Morgan, the FBI man, who finally cracked the door. Griffin and Dr. Kent were with him.

"You all right?" asked Morgan.

"I'm fine," MacHeath said, "but Bern is going to have a sore neck for a while. I didn't hit him hard enough to break it, but he'll get plenty of sleep before he wakes up."

More FBI men came in, and they dragged out the unprotesting Bern.

Dr. Kent said: "Well, I'm glad that's over. I'll have to get back and see what Dr. Nordred is raving about."

"Raving?" asked MacHeath innocently.

"Yes. While I was in the pump room reducing the pressure, he called me on the interphone. Said he'd been looking all over for me. He and Luvochek and Bessermann are up in the lab." He frowned. "They claim that one of the radiolead samples was floating in the air in the lab. It's settled down now, I gather, but it only weighs a fraction of what it should, though it's gaining all the time. And that's ridiculous. It's not at all what Dr. Nordred's theory predicted." Then he clamped his lips together, thinking perhaps he had talked too much.

"Interesting," said MacHeath blandly. "Very interesting."

*S*enator Gonzales sat in Brian Taggert's sixth-floor office in the S.M.M.R. building and looked puzzled. "All right, I grant you that Bern couldn't have been the saboteur. Then why arrest him?"

Dave MacHeath took a drag from his cigarette before he answered. "We had to have a patsy — someone to put the blame on. No one really believed that it was just bad luck, but they'll all accept the idea that Bern was a saboteur."

"We would have had to arrest him eventually, anyway," said Brian Taggert.

"Give me a quick run-down," Gonzales said. "I've got to explain this to the President."

"Did you ever hear of the Pauli Effect?" MacHeath asked.

"Something about the number of electrons that —"

"No," MacHeath said quickly. "That's the Pauli *principle*, better known as the Exclusion Principle. The Pauli *Effect* is a different thing entirely, a psionic effect.

"It used to be said that a theoretical physicist was judged by his inability to handle research apparatus; the clumsier he was in research, the better he was with theory. But Wolfgang Pauli was a lot more than clumsy. Apparatus would break, topple over, go to pieces, or burn up if Pauli just walked into the room.

"Up to the time he died, in 1958, his colleagues kidded about it, without really believing there was anything behind it. But it is recorded that the explosion of some vacuum equipment in a laboratory at the University of Göttingen was the direct result of the Pauli Effect. It was definitely established that the explosion occurred at the precise moment that a train on which Pauli was traveling stopped for a short time at the Göttingen railway station."

The senator said: "The poltergeist phenomenon."

"Not exactly," MacHeath said, "although there is a similarity. The poltergeist phenomenon is usually spectacular and is nearly always associated with teen-age neurotics. Then there's the pyrotic; fires always start in his vicinity."

"But there's always a reason for psionic phenomena to react violently under subconscious control," Senator Gonzales pointed out. "There's always a psychological quirk."

"Sure. And I almost fell into the same trap, myself."

"How so?"

"I was thinking that if Bern were the saboteur, all our theories about psionics would have to be thrown out — we'd have to start from a different set of precepts. *And I didn't even want to think about such an idea!*"

"Nobody likes their pet theories overthrown," Gonzales observed.

"Of course not. But here's the point: The only way that a scientific theory can be proved wrong is to uncover a phenomenon which doesn't fit in with the theory. A theoretical physicist is a mathematician; he makes logical deductions and logical predictions by juggling symbols around in accordance with some logical system. But the axioms, the assumptions upon which those systems are built, are nonlogical. You can't prove an axiom; if comes right out of the mind.

"So imagine that you're a theoretical physicist. A really original-type thinker. You come up with a mathematical system that explains all known phenomena at that time, and predicts others that are, as yet, unknown. You check your math over and over again; there's no error in your logic, since it all follows, step by step."

"Okay; go on," Gonzales said interestedly.

"Very well, then; you've built yourself a logical universe, based on your axioms, and the structure seems to have a one-to-one correspondence with the actual universe. Not only that, but if the theory is accepted, you've built your reputation on it — your life.

"Now, what happens if your axioms — not the logic *about* the axioms, but the axioms themselves — are proven to be wrong?"

*B*rian Taggert took his pipe out of his mouth. "Why, you give up the erroneous set of axioms and build a new set that will explain the new phenomenon. Isn't that what a scientist is supposed to do?" His manner was that of wide-eyed innocence laid on with a large trowel.

"Oh, *sure* it is," said the senator. "A man builds his whole life, his whole universe; on a set of principles, and he scraps them at the drop of a hat. *Sure* he does."

"He claims he will," MacHeath said. "Any scientist worth the paper his diploma is printed on is firmly convinced that he will change his axioms as soon as they're proven false. Of course, ninety-nine percent of 'em *can't* and *won't* and *don't*. They refuse to look at anything that suggests changing axioms.

"Some scientists eagerly accept the axioms that they were taught in school and hang on to them all their lives, fighting change tooth and nail. Oh, they'll accept new ideas, all right — provided that they fit in with the structures based on the old axioms.

"Then there are the young iconoclasts who don't like the axioms as they stand, so they make up some new ones of their own — men like Newton, Einstein, Planck, and so on. Then, once the new axioms have been forced down the throats of their colleagues, the innovators become the Old Order; the iconoclasts become the ones who put the fences around the new images to safeguard them. And they're even more firmly wedded to their axioms than anyone else. This is *their* universe!

"Of course, these men proclaim to all the world that they are perfectly willing to change their axioms. And the better a scientist he is, the more he believes, in his heart-of-hearts, that he really would change. He really thinks, consciously, that he wants others to test his theories.

"But notice: A theory is only good if it explains all known phenomena in its field. If it does, then the only thing that can topple it is a *new* fact. The only thing that can threaten the complex structure formulated by a really creative, painstaking, mathematical physicist is *experiment!*"

Senator Gonzales' attentive silence was eloquent.

"Experiment!" MacHeath repeated. "That can wreck a theory quicker and more completely than all the learned arguments of a dozen men. And every theoretician is aware of that fact. Consciously, he gladly accepts the inevitable; but his subconscious mind will fight to keep those axioms.

"Even if it has to smash every experimental device around!

"After all, if nobody can experiment on your theory, it can't be proved wrong, can it?

"In Nordred's case, as in Pauli's, this subconscious defense actually made itself felt in the form of broken equipment. Dr. Theodore Nordred was totally unconscious of the fact that he detested and feared the idea of anyone experimenting to prove or disprove his theory. He had no idea that he, himself, was re-channeling the energy in those machines to make them burn out."

Brian Taggert looked at MacHeath pointedly. "Do you think the shock treatment you gave him will cause any repercussions?"

"No. Griffin and Benbow held that block of radiolead floating in the air only while Dr. Nordred was alone in the lab. He pushed at it, felt of it, and moved it around for more than ten minutes before he'd admit the reality of what he saw. Then he called Luvochek and Bessermann in to look at it.

"Griffin and Benbow let the sample settle to the desk, so that by the time the other two scientists got to the lab, the lead didn't have an apparent negative weight, but was still much lighter than it should be.

"All the while that Bessermann and Luvochek were trying to weigh the lead block, to get an accurate measurement, Griffin and Benbow, three rooms away, kept increasing the weight slowly towards normal. And so far no one has invented a device which will give an instantaneous check on the weight of an object. A balance can't check the weight of a sample unless that weight is constant; there's too much time lag involved.

"So, what evidence do they have? Scientifically speaking, none. They have no measurements, and the experiment can't be repeated. And only Nordred actually saw the sample *float-*

ing. Luvochek and Bessermann will eventually think up a 'natural' explanation for the apparent steady gain in weight. Only Nordred will remain convinced that what he saw actually happened.

"I don't see how there could be any serious repercussions in the field of physics." But he looked at Taggert for confirmation.

Taggert gave it to him with an approving look.

"It's a funny thing," said Gonzales musingly. "Some time back, we were in a situation where we had to go to the extreme of physical violence to keep from demonstrating to a scientist that psionic powers could be controlled, just to keep from ruining the physicist's work.

"Now, we turn right around and demonstrate the 'impossible' to another physicist in order to pull his hard-earned axioms out from under him." He smiled wryly. "There ain't no justice in the world."

"No," agreed MacHeath, "but the trick worked. He won't have any subconscious desire to smash equipment just to protect a theory that has already been smashed. On the contrary, he'll let them go through in order to find new data to build another theory on."

"He'll never again be the man he was," said Taggert regretfully. "He's lost the force of his convictions. He won't be capable of taking a no-nonsense, dogmatic, black-and-white stand. But it was necessary." He made an odd gesture with one hand. "What else can you do with a man who's a psionic psychopath?"

THE END

www.ingramcontent.com/pod-product-compliance
Lightning Source LLC
Chambersburg PA
CBHW031905170626
46807CB00004B/1909